Kidnap

Chris Powling

**For Jake, Polly, Suzie and Joe
whenever they're ready**

First published 2011 by A & C Black,
an imprint of Bloomsbury Publishing Plc
50 Bedford Square, London WC1B 3DP

www.acblack.com

ISBN 978-1-4081-4260-8

A CIP catalogue for this book is available from the British Library.

Printed and bound in Great Britain
by CPI Cox and Wyman, Reading, RG1 8EX

recommended by

www.catchup.org

Catch Up is a not-for-profit charity which
aims to address the problem of
underachievement that has its roots in
literacy and numeracy difficulties.

Contents

Chapter 1

Gunmen

It was a hot sticky afternoon, and something bad was about to happen.

I just knew it. I felt it with every tick of the clock. It was like waiting for a bomb to go off. I was so jumpy I let out a groan.

Our private teacher looked up from her marking. "Day-dreaming again, Adam?" she asked.

"Me, Miss Archer?" I said.

"Well, I'm not talking about Leo," she snapped. "He's working as hard as he always does. So is your little sister, come to that. Is the story going well, Daisy?"

"Fine, Miss," grinned Daisy.

"And how about yours, Leo?" asked Miss Archer.

"Pretty well, Miss," Leo mumbled.

"Well, I hope it's as good as your last story," said Miss Archer. "It might even give Adam some ideas."

Leo bit his lip. He hated it when Miss Archer praised him instead of us. I hated it, too.

My little sister and I were rich kids, you see. And Leo was a poor kid. He was the son of Mr Kilby, who did odd jobs around the house.

Mum and Dad's latest mad idea was to let Leo join us and have private lessons.

"It'll be good for all three of you," they'd told us.

So far, it had been good for Leo. You should have seen his work-outs in our gym. Or his racing dives in our swimming pool. He was even brilliant at riding our quad bike.

"Look at him go!" Daisy had yelled. "He's so cool!"

"Cooler than me?" I asked.

"Not that cool, Adam…" she muttered.

"You reckon?" I said.

My little sister had nodded quickly. But I knew she was just being kind. Leo was better than me at everything we did. And that included writing stories.

I glared down at my empty page. I had to write *something*, so I began:

Something bad is about to happen. I …

My writing came to a stop.

What was that noise?

I looked up and saw that Leo and Daisy were listening, too. So was Miss Archer. We could hear a faint scratching noise. It was like a sheet of glass being cut. But how could it be that? Why hadn't the alarm gone off?

Daisy caught her breath. "Miss…" she said.

"Look!" Leo gasped.

Outside the window was a man in a black track suit. His trainers, gloves and ski-mask were also black. So was his shiny, snub-nosed gun. It was aimed at Miss Archer.

"Just do what I say, Teacher Lady," he said.

He slipped through the gap in the glass. Behind him came three more men in black. They lined up behind us as if they knew exactly what to do.

Each of them carried a shiny, snub-nosed gun.

I felt Daisy's hand grab mine. No one said a word. Our private mansion, in its private park, with its private school-room and private security system, was supposed to keep us safe. This was the worst nightmare a rich kid can have.

Chapter 2

On the Money

It was the first man who did the talking. His ski-mask muffled his voice a bit. "Do as I say, Teacher Lady," he said, "and nobody will get hurt."

Miss Archer's mouth was a narrow slit.

"You'll never get away with this," she hissed.

"Won't we?" he laughed.

He tilted his gun. It wasn't snub-nosed any more.

"See this thing on my gun?" he said. "It's called a silencer. One squeeze of the trigger and there's a pop like a tiny balloon. That's all the noise it makes. So do exactly as you're told, Teacher Lady. If anything upsets me – anything at all – it'll be pop-pop-pop-pop. Remember, I'm the Boss Man here."

The Boss Man smiled. At least, I think that's what he did. It was hard to tell because most of his face was hidden by the ski-mask.

"In a kidnap, you're worth money alive *or* dead," he said. "People just need to *think* they can get you back alive, and they pay up. So don't upset me."

"How much money do you want?" I asked.

"For you and your little sister?" he said.

"For all four of us," said Daisy, quickly. "Mum and Dad will pay for Leo and Miss Archer, too."

Now I was sure he had a smile on his face. He lowered the gun and moved quickly across the school-room. When he reached Daisy and me, he stopped.

"Well now," he said. "Let's work out a price, shall we? For a couple of rich kids like you, I'd say about ten million pounds each. For that Teacher Lady, I'll take a thousand pounds. But now comes the tricky bit. Who's this little lad you've got with you? What's your name?"

"Leo Kilby."

"And who are you?" asked the Boss Man.

"My dad's the odd job man," said Leo.

"Here at the house?"

"That's right," Leo said.

"Been here long, has he?" said the Boss Man.

"Pretty long, yes."

"It's good to hear that, Leo, because me and my men are doing our best to keep him in work. There's the broken window, and a chunk of wall that needs re-building. Then there are all the trip-wires and alarm bells we had to cut. Can your dad mend stuff like that?"

Leo looked up at the Boss Man.

"I think so."

"Tell you what, then," said the Boss Man. "We have given your dad a lot of work, so we won't make a charge for you. We'll let you go for free – when we have the money for the others. Now, I can't say fairer than that, can I?"

"Thanks," Leo said.

What came next was more team-work. All it took was a nod from the Boss Man. The other three men put their guns under their track suits and pushed us through the window, down the ladder and across the back lawn.

There were no trip-wires to snag in the grass now. No alarm bells to go off. Even the hole in the wall was easy to miss if it wasn't you who'd made it.

Parked in the lane outside was a white van. They pushed us into it.

I looked at my watch. The kidnap had taken less than eleven minutes.

They had timed it perfectly. Half the house staff were on holiday. Mum and Dad had been up in the city all week. Even Major Vincent, our Head of Security, was away today. So far so good, then, for the men in ski-masks.

And so far so bad for us.

Chapter 3

Pop-Pop-Pop

The back of the van was dark and stuffy. The only light came from a small window in the roof. We could hardly see each other, let alone the three men on the bench facing us. One of them was the Boss Man.

He rapped on the metal grill which shut us off from the fourth man in the driver's cab. The van moved off at once.

The Boss Man took out a pack of cigarettes. He offered one to Miss Archer.

"Smoke?" he asked.

"No thank you. It's a dirty habit," replied Miss Archer.

"Please yourself," said the Boss Man, but he sounded cross.

He turned to Daisy. "How about you?" he asked. "Do you fancy a fag?"

"Me?" said my little sister.

"Why not?" said the Boss Man. "You don't have to do what Teacher Lady says.

None of you do. Not any more. You see, she thinks she's still in charge. But she isn't. Do you know who is?"

"You?" Daisy whispered.

"That's right," said the Boss Man.

He looked over at Leo and me. "We *all* know who's in charge, do we?"

"You," I managed to say.

"You," Leo added.

"That's good to hear. We're all agreed. Well, almost all. How about you, Teacher Lady?"

Miss Archer looked like she might cry. I held my breath, waiting for her reply.

The Boss Man was waiting, too.

He lit his cigarette. It dangled from the slit in his ski-mask.

"Make your mind up now, Teacher Lady," he growled. "Who's in charge round here?"

"You are," said Miss Archer quietly.

"Say it louder," snarled the Boss Man.

"You are," repeated Miss Archer.

But she'd spoken much too sharply. Nobody in the van believed her – least of all the Boss Man. The cigarette jiggled in his mouth. "Right answer," he said. "But wrong tone of voice."

He reached under his track suit. Out came the gun with its silencer. He tapped it three times on the grill.

This must have been a signal because the van slowed to a halt. "Open the door," he ordered. "Let's see what's outside."

"Here, Boss?" asked the driver.

"It's as good a place as any," laughed the Boss Man.

Everyone blinked in the bright light as the van's door swung back. "Trees, Boss. Some kind of forest," said the driver.

"Perfect," smiled the Boss Man.

He turned to Miss Archer. "Out," he said.

"What?" whispered Miss Archer. She was as white as a sheet.

"Out!" snarled the Boss Man.

"Look," said Miss Archer. "I won't..."

"Stop talking and listen to me. This is your last chance. I'll give you five minutes' start, okay? Five full minutes to run as fast as you can. You should be well out of range by then. After that, I'll follow. If I catch up with you…"

"You'll shoot me?" whispered Miss Archer.

The Boss Man closed an eye and looked at her along the barrel of the gun. "I can shoot you right here if you like," he said.

Miss Archer was sitting very still. Daisy and I had never liked her. She was far too strict. But we were sorry for her now. Could she really get away with a five-minute start?

No way, I'd have said. She'd be mad even to try. On the other hand, what choice had she got?

We watched, hardly daring to breathe, as she got out of the van. I smelled her lavender perfume as she brushed by me.

"Good luck, kids," she called over her shoulder. "I'll do my best – "

"Shut up, Teacher Lady," said the Boss Man.

"I was just – " said Miss Archer.

"Shut up!"

With the end of his gun, he prodded our teacher on her way. We heard her start to run through the trees.

The Boss Man took a careful, two-handed aim. He was right about the silencer: pop-pop-pop.

After that came a scream, a sound of falling, and then silence.

The Boss Man spat out his cigarette. "I lied about the five minutes," he said.

None of us said a word – not the other men in ski-masks, not Daisy, not Leo, not me. But I did notice the look on Leo's face just before the van door banged shut on us again. OK, it was as stunned as Daisy's and mine. But he didn't seem surprised. I felt my heart skip a beat. Had Leo been expecting something like this?

Chapter 4

Tower Block

The van ride seemed to last forever. We had three stops in all – one of them for food and the others for toilet breaks.

"Don't get me upset, kids," the Boss Man said every time we pulled up. "You've seen what happens if I get upset: pop-pop-pop."

He grinned and patted the gun under his armpit. "Make that Teacher Lady proud, OK? I'd hate to think the old bat died in vain."

"Did you *have* to kill her?" Daisy said.

"No," said the Boss Man.

"So why did you?" asked Daisy.

"Because she upset me," he replied.

So we were very careful not to upset him when he let us out of the van.

It was dusk when we reached the city centre. We parked outside the tallest, darkest tower block I'd ever seen. It rose up and up – about 50 floors of sky-high brick and steel. I could have counted at least a thousand windows. But not one of them was lit.

The Boss Man was grinning again.

"Welcome home," he said.

"Home?" I said.

"It will be when it opens next week," the
Boss Man said with a laugh.

"I don't get it," I said.

"This place belongs to your dad," said
Leo, softly.

I heard Daisy gasp quietly. We knew at
once he was right. But how come Leo knew
it? What else did he know about my family?

We slipped through a side door and were
pushed into a lift. Don't ask me how high
we went. All I remember is making my way
through the top floor flat, which opened onto a
big balcony.

At least the night air cleared my head.

The Boss Man was already setting up his deal with Mum and Dad.

"Twenty million for the two of them," he said in his hard, flat voice. "We'll throw in the other lad for free."

He held out the mobile phone to me and Daisy. "Say something to your dad," he snapped. "He thinks I'm bluffing."

"It's all true, Dad," I yelled.

"He shot Miss Archer in the back," Daisy added. "He said he'd give her a five-minute start but he was lying."

"Got that?" said the Boss Man.

He had the phone clamped to his ear again.

"And don't try to be clever," he growled. "You'll never trace this call. You'll never find your two kids, either. At least, not while they're still alive. Do everything I've said and get the twenty million together. I'll ring you later with details of the pick-up."

"What's that?" he went on. "Oh, your mother wants a word…"

He tilted the phone towards us.

"Your mum's crying her eyes out, kids. Why not blow her a goodnight kiss?"

He was just winding us up. With a flip of his wrist he tossed the phone over the balcony. It fell, but we never heard it hit the ground.

"Happy landings," grinned one of the men.

"On a cop, with any luck," smiled another man. "The poor old plod will never know what hit him."

The Boss Man sent his team indoors. "No need for you to come in yet," he told us. "Why not stay out here and plan an escape bid? Do you want to know where to find the only exit?"

"The exit?" Daisy blinked.

"It's over there," he said.

He jerked his thumb where the phone had gone. For all we knew it was still falling through the air. Would our mum be listening when it smashed to bits on the pavement?

Chapter 5

Leo Makes His Move

We stared at each other in silence for a moment. Above us, a full moon blotted out the stars.

"Let's go indoors," Daisy shivered.

"Not yet," Leo said. "We need to talk."

"We can talk inside, can't we?" I said.

"Not if they've bugged the room," Leo said. "They can't bug a balcony – not a balcony as big as this one."

I shrugged. "If you say so."

Leo had a far-away look on his face. He looked up.

"This is the penthouse, isn't it?" he said. "It was hard to tell on the way up. But see how this wall slopes back? We must be on the top floor."

"So what?" I said.

"So there's only the roof above us. And it'll be linked up with some kind of outside fire escape, I bet," said Leo.

"Is there normally a fire escape down from the roof?" I asked.

"Your dad would insist on it, surely, Adam. He built these flats, after all, and he's a bit of a fusspot, isn't he? He always puts safety first."

"What makes you say that?" I asked.

"My dad told me," said Leo.

"Your dad, the odd-job man?" I said, coldly. "What does *he* know?"

"Adam!" Daisy exclaimed.

Okay, so I was out of order. The thing was, Leo was right. Our dad *was* a bit of a safety-first fusspot.

That wasn't the problem. The problem was that I was getting to know Leo. He really was cool. He was so cool he made me sick. No, not sick – suspicious. I'd seen him swimming in our pool and working out in our gym. I'd seen the way he rode our quad bike.

Where had a kid like him, with a dad who did odd jobs, learned to do so much cool stuff? And how did he know so much about our dad?

But Daisy didn't think there was anything odd about Leo. She just stared at him with the biggest goo-goo eyes I've ever seen.

"Can you find this fire escape, Leo?" she asked. "Will it really get us out of here?"

"Well, I can't be sure…" said Leo.

"You can't be sure?" I said. "And you're acting like our leader? What kind of an answer is that?"

Leo pulled a face. "It's an honest answer, Adam. It's the only answer I've got. But I can tell you what *won't* save us."

"Go on, then," I snarled.

"Doing nothing at all," said Leo, looking at me.

As Leo was talking to us, he was running his hands over the brick wall. He felt it all the way along to the corner of the balcony. "Got it!" he said.

"Got what?" I asked.

"I've found the first step," said Leo.

Leo swung himself up. One slip now and he'd plunge past 49 other balconies, till the ground split him apart like an egg you've dropped on the kitchen floor.

Daisy gave a cry of fear. "Leo?" she croaked.

"Shush!" said Leo.

"Leo, I can't see you!" called Daisy.

"I'm here on the fire escape. Honestly, it's dead clever – like a set of steps chipped into the line of the roof. Looks a bit tricky, though. Stay where you are till I've checked it out," whispered Leo.

"Suppose the kidnappers come back?" asked Daisy.

"Tell them I fell," Leo said.

He was as swift and silent as a cat as he vanished into the night. Soon, there wasn't a sound from the level above us. The Boss Man himself couldn't have made a quicker getaway.

The Boss Man...

That got me thinking. Were Leo and the Boss Man alike in other ways? Yes, they were. They had the same confidence, didn't they? The same skills. Even the same sort of training, for all I knew. How come I hadn't spotted this before?

"There's something fishy going on here," I said.

"Fishy?" asked Daisy. "What do you mean?"

"With Leo," I went on. "Is he really on our side? Or is he part of the Boss Man's team? Maybe he's just left us to join them."

"But his dad's our odd-job man, Adam!" said Daisy.

"Exactly," I said. "Think about it. Who looks after all the trip wires and the alarm bells back in the grounds at home?"

"Leo's dad," said Daisy.

"And who keeps an eye on all the windows and all the other security stuff – including the outside wall?" I asked.

"Leo's dad…" Daisy said again.

"Can't you see a pattern?" I said.

"No," said Daisy, and she turned away from me.

"Daisy, it's a no-brainer. Leo's dad knows our house from top to bottom. He knows everything that goes on in the place. He knows when Dad and Mum have gone away and half the staff are on holiday. He knows when Major Vincent is away."

I went on. "The kidnap was so easy, wasn't it? Much *too* easy. There had to be an insider … someone who was feeding all the facts to the Boss Man."

"And you think that was Leo's dad?" said Daisy.

"Daisy, they're both on the Boss Man's team – Leo *and* his dad!"

"No," said Daisy, firmly.

"Okay." I shrugged. "Prove me wrong."

Daisy didn't say another word. She just stared at me long and hard. Then she made *her* move. She was as swift and silent as Leo.

At the corner of the balcony, she swung herself onto the steps built into the roof. After that, just like Leo, she vanished.

Chapter 6

On the Up

So I followed her.

What else could I do? When your kid sister does something like that, you don't have a lot of choice – not that high in the sky. Not when the Boss Man might return at any moment.

Thank goodness for the moonlight on the staircase. It showed me my next hand-hold and where to put my feet.

Also, it hid how far there was to fall if we lost our grip.

Suppose Daisy fell? Would I have the strength to grab her? Or would we both drop down like stones with one last scream on our lips?

I didn't want to think about that. To tell the truth, I didn't want to think about anything. My best bet was to focus on the stairway.

"Are you still up there, Daisy?" I called.

No answer.

I felt totally alone. How far was there still to go? Had Daisy reached the top yet?

Up and up I climbed.

Suddenly, I bumped against a low wall. I went forward on my hands and knees. I was on the very top of the building. Ahead of me was flatness. Nothing but flatness.

"This must be…" I began.

"…a helicopter pad," someone said.

"Daisy?" I whispered.

I hadn't noticed her in the darkness. She put a finger to her lips and pointed.

Leo hadn't seen us, either. He was crouching in the shadow of some cabins about fifty feet away.

He seemed to be talking into his sleeve.

"He's wired up," I snarled. "He's speaking to his mates in the ski-masks."

"That's rubbish!" said Daisy.

"Is it? Remember all that stuff about our room being bugged? It's Leo who's wearing the bug! He's helping the kidnappers keep track of us."

"Adam, you're – "

That was as far as Daisy got. She was so angry she'd started to turn and walk away from me as she spoke.

She must have forgotten the low wall behind her. I saw her panic as she tripped and lost her balance. Then she fell off the roof.

Chapter 7

Over the Edge

Split a split-second, okay…

Now split the split.

That's how fast I got to Daisy. With one hand I gripped the rim of that smooth, bare rooftop. With the other I grabbed the neck of her shirt. My arm was nearly jerked out of its socket. Yet somehow I held her fast. I knew this because I could hear my sister choking.

That was all my fault. Instead of saving my sister I was strangling her.

I almost dropped her.

I almost *had* to drop her. She was too heavy for me. I could feel my hand slipping.

"Adam!" Daisy tried to call. "Adam!"

"Daisy!" I yelled.

It sounded like a last goodbye. Should I hold on or let her go?

Whatever I did, my little sister would die.

Then a pair of arms locked around my waist.

They were far stronger than mine. "Don't lose your grip," hissed a voice. "She'll be fine when she's up here again."

"Drag us back if you can," I wheezed.

"That's what I'm doing," said Leo.

Now I didn't have to hold the wall any more, I could use both hands on Daisy's shirt, so she could breathe. Inch by inch, gasp by gasp, the three of us edged back on the roof.

"It's okay, sis," I told her as we pulled her over the low wall.

She fell on her hands and knees beside me. Then she was suddenly sick.

"Shock, probably," I said.

And then I was sick myself.

Shock, probably.

Leo didn't look the least bit shocked. He stared down at us, hands on hips. A tell-tale loop of wire drooped from his sleeve. I gave a bitter grin when I saw it.

"Everything under control?" I sneered.

"Not yet," Leo said.

"Adam! He's just saved our lives!" said Daisy.

"He's just saved his mates twenty million quid, more like," I snarled.

"Do you really believe that?" Leo sighed.

"Tell me why I shouldn't," I said.

For the first time ever I saw him hesitate. I really thought I'd got him.

Then he rolled back his sleeve. Strapped to the inside of his wrist was a tiny bit of kit no bigger than a hearing-aid.

"You were right, Adam," he said. "I've been hiding something all along. This links me with Major Vincent."

"Major Vincent?" I said.

Leo nodded. "He got wind of this kidnap months ago. Something was odd about it, though … something he couldn't put his finger on."

Leo went on, "So he asked my dad if he could give me some basic security training just in case. That's why I joined your lessons this summer."

"And your dad agreed to let you do it?" I said.

"He was in the army with Major Vincent," said Leo.

"So why didn't you tell us all this before?" I asked.

"Because you might have given the game away by mistake. I've been talking to the Major whenever I could – at each of the places we stopped. We spoke only a moment ago. He's sending a police helicopter with an armed response unit. They should be here in fifteen minutes."

"Can we keep clear of the Boss Man till then?" asked Daisy.

"We've got to," said Leo. "The Major says we must stay close by till the helicopter picks us up. That may not be so easy."

Leo didn't need to explain. On one side of us was the line of cabins. The rest of the roof – *most* of the roof – was as empty as a football pitch stripped of its turf.

As a place to view the city it was fine, but as a place to hide, it sucked.

Chapter 8

Top of the World

So we went to the cabins. Where else could we go? Leo led the way with Daisy close behind him.

I hung back a bit. I was ashamed of myself for getting it all so wrong.

That was, if I *had* got it wrong.

At the back of my mind I was still uneasy. The kidnap itself had been so simple. No snags with our security system. No problems with the family timetable.

Somebody in the house must have been tipping off the kidnappers.

If it wasn't Leo's dad, who was it? Who was the last member of the Boss Man's team?

We stopped at the nearest cabin. Its sliding doors stood wide open. Leo edged through the gap.

"Can't see anybody," he said.

"Is it a good place to hide?" Daisy asked.

"Maybe," said Leo quietly.

It was some kind of store room. There were bins, shelves and metal racks down the middle of the room and on all the four walls around us. The place was crammed with tools and cleaning kit.

"Must be for the whole tower block," said Leo.

"Why are the doors wide open?" I whispered. "And who's turned on the lights?"

"That's what I was wondering," muttered Leo.

He lifted a finger to his lips. He was listening.

Then Daisy and I heard it, too – the sound of quiet voices from the far end of the store room.

One of them was hard and flat: the Boss
Man. Was he giving the others their orders?

Daisy glanced at the sliding doors. On
one of them hung a padlock as big as a fist. I
saw her eyes light up.

"If we slam the doors right now and snap
the padlock into place..." she whispered.

"We'd have them trapped," I said.

"Brilliant," said Leo.

He stepped back outside the cabin and
pulled us into a huddle.

"We've got to be sure they're all in there,"
he hissed. "Give me a minute to find that out.
Daisy, check outside the cabin for other exits."

He looked at me.

"Adam, if I don't come back … padlock the door anyway. After that, find the lift or staircase that brought them up here."

He was gone before I could argue. My sister, too. It was the longest minute of my life. Panic makes you feel like that. So does worry.

If the Boss Man's team did capture Leo, what would I do? What if they got their hands on Daisy?

When Daisy tapped my arm a moment later, I almost jumped out of my skin.

"No other exits," she said.

"And all four of them are in the cabin," added Leo, behind me.

"Did you count them?" I asked.

"About a million times," said Leo.

"Quick, Adam!" said Daisy.

I grabbed both the doors and pulled hard. They slid together. The padlock gave a sharp click as I hooked it shut.

"Test it," said Leo.

"Locked solid," I told him.

"Got 'em!" he beamed.

Daisy bumped against me but she wasn't looking at me or Leo. She was staring across the roof. Her face was white and blank, and now Leo's face went pale, too.

"Another kidnapper?" he gasped. "I don't believe it!"

"You'd better believe it," I said.

After all, I'd believed it myself almost from the start.

The fifth member of the Boss Man's team had just stepped onto the rooftop. Dressed all in black, of course. With a ski-mask as a disguise. And holding a shiny, snub-nosed gun.

Chapter 9

In for the Kill

The Boss Man had trained his team well. This guy seemed smaller than the others but just as mean. He used the same two-handed grip on the gun.

No silencer, I noticed. Why would a gun need a silencer at the top of an empty tower block?

Crack!

A puff of dust spat back from the cabin doors. Had the kidnapper missed us on purpose? Maybe it was intended as a warning. Leo recovered first.

"Hey!" he called out. "The ransom money gets paid for these two. I'm worth nothing. Keep your gun trained on me."

"Leo!" cried Daisy.

"He's right, Daisy," I said.

My sister gave me a nasty look. I didn't care. What Leo had said was true.

And he'd got the kidnapper's full attention. This helped me move a couple of steps away from the line of fire.

Daisy didn't try to get away. She edged closer to Leo. As he tried to push her away, I took another step out of danger.

I needed the gun to stay on Leo a little longer. Then I could make my run.

Had Leo worked out what I was up to? I saw his eyes flick towards me. Then back at the snub-nosed gun.

"You need to pick a target," he shouted to the kidnapper. "You can't shoot three of us at once."

No, but we could be shot one by one if we stayed close together. I needed to take another step to widen the gap between us. But would it make me the target if I did? Was I brave enough to do it?

Crack!

No puff of dust this time. Instead the bullet skimmed the padlock and pinged off into the night. So *that* was the target. And the first direct hit would smash it to pieces. Inside the cabin there was a sound of shouting and banging fists.

But not for long.

When a helicopter arrives you hear nothing but the sound of the helicopter.

The noise was deafening. The blades seemed to shred the air. Next came the search-light – every square inch of the space was lit up. If I hadn't shut my eyes in time, I'd have been blind as well as deaf.

By then I'd grabbed my chance. I raced over the roof as fast as I'd ever run.

"Aiyeeeeee!" I yelled, and I threw myself at the kidnapper.

I was pretty much in mid-air as my head hit the kidnapper in the belly. We fell onto the tarmac, one on top of the other. That's when I smelled the scent of lavender.

"Lavender?" I said.

"You little brute!" the kidnapper spat.

"Miss Archer!" I gasped.

Crack!

I'd forgotten her shiny, snub-nosed gun.
As I stared through the ski-mask into our
teacher's hate-filled eyes, I felt no pain at all.
The pain came a moment later, just before I
blacked out.

Chapter 10

Last Words

The smell of flowers woke me up. They were all round my hospital bed – roses, tulips, lilies. "What, no lavender?" I said.

"Didn't think you'd want it!" someone said.

"Daisy?" I called.

"Yes I'm here, and Leo's here too. We talked Mum and Dad into letting us be your first visitors."

"Miss Archer says sorry that she couldn't make it." Leo grinned. "She's in the nick with the other kidnappers."

"So she *was* the insider!" I said.

"She was, and the police think she's their leader, too. We should have been thinking Boss Lady, not Boss Man. Even Major Vincent didn't work that out. She faked her own death so nobody would suspect her."

"You're lucky you've only got a flesh wound," Daisy said.

"The police jumped out of the helicopter so fast they nearly landed on both of you. They're amazed we were still alive. They called us heroes."

"Heroes?" I said.

"That's what they say," laughed Leo.

"That's what everybody says," beamed Daisy. "The media's gone mad. We're all over the press, the radio and TV!"

After that we sat and talked, trying to feel like heroes. But we couldn't keep it up. Sooner or later, one of us had a fit of the giggles. Then my leg began to throb. The Ward Sister told Daisy and Leo to go away so I could get some sleep.

Just before they left, though, they gave me the best news of all. Next term, I'll be joining Leo at the local school. So will Daisy when she's old enough. After what happened with our private lessons this summer, the new plan is to go for 'safety in numbers'.

That's Major Vincent's advice, anyway. Mum and Dad are still thinking it over, but I'm pretty sure he'll get them to agree. After all, we may be a couple of rich kids but we won't ever be on our own. Not with two thousand other kids around us. And not with the best possible back-up from the coolest kid of the lot … our good friend, Leo Kilby.